MOUNTAIN BRIDE

Mountain Bride

AN INCREDIBLE TALE BY

Elizabeth Coatsworth

Illustrations by George W. Thompson

PANTHEON

FOR
KATE AND MARGARET
whose patient listening
helped the book to take form

FOREWORD

PETE FORTIER and his family are imaginary, and
I have taken liberties with Time and Space:
with Time in adding a season to the three during which the Fortiers would normally be at
their cabin; with Space in shortening some of
the distances. The rest of the tale is based on
Indian legends, still current and still so alive
that their form is constantly being renewed by
the people of the region, as I have tried to renew
it in the following pages.

I am deeply indebted to my friend, Maurice

7

Day, who goes each autumn camping and painting in the Katahdin wilderness, and returns with sketches and tales which I have enjoyed over the years. He and his wife have been kind enough to read the manuscript, and must more than once have smiled to find his experiences caught up in the story of Sylvia.

—E. C.

MOUNTAIN BRIDE

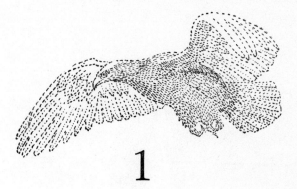

1

THE APRIL rain was falling lightly. The drops tapped on the roof of the ranger's cabin with a rustling insistence, and ran murmuring down the windowpanes. Among the trees, the sound had a faint sibilance, and far above, shrouded in mist, the showers fell endlessly on the great granite slides and ridges of hidden Katahdin, and finding a million accustomed veinings, drew downwards into Katahdin Stream, deepening its course and adding to the wild exultance of the falls and the white rush

13

and music of its passage at the foot of the cabin's clearing.

Pete Fortier had enough Indian blood in him to hear everything, even as he sat at his desk by the window making out a report on the steps he had recently taken in finding a pair of lost campers. He made no mention in this report or in any other of the fact that his only child, Sylvia, had disappeared twelve days earlier, leaving almost no trace behind her.

Now as he finished his writing he glanced out of the window, and a slight movement, more than that of the spray carried along above Katahdin Stream, caught his eye. His glance focused sharply. He was all attention like an animal, and although he made no sound or motion of any kind, his wife, crocheting in her rocking chair nearer the fire, was aware that something had happened. She looked up from her work.

"Pete?"

"Did you want something, dear?" he asked in his usual voice, folding the papers on which he had been at work. Then unhurriedly he put them into a long envelope, sealed and stamped

14

it, and placed it neatly parallel to the edge of his desk.

"There's one more report on its way to headquarters," he added, looking at her with a smile.

"It was about the men you found yesterday?"

"Yes."

"But you didn't find——?"

"No. There was no trace of Sylvie. And yet I feel quite certain that we shall see her soon."

Now he had his wife's full attention.

"*See* her?" she asked, her voice beginning to tremble. "But before this, you've thought that she was, that she was alive but, but——" her voice trailed off. Then she began again.

"Have you had word from Tom Ellison?" she asked with a faint eagerness.

"No, no. I've told you that Tom Ellison has had nothing to do with Sylvie's going."

"But surely she wouldn't go off into the woods like that all alone! A girl of seventeen and so pretty——"

"Perhaps we'll know later. But I feel more and more certain that we shall see her soon."

"Is it just one of your presentiments, Pete, or something you're really sure of?"

She had gone very white and he smiled back at her reassuringly, steadying her as he had so often steadied her in the past.

"No," he said, and now he swung his chair around from the desk, so that he faced her. "It's not a presentiment this time, Ethel. My presentiment was that we would not hear from Sylvie for a long time. Perhaps never. But that she was alive. I was wrong again, for she is on her way home."

The woman's face had gone old, but she kept hold of herself. Her hands were no longer shaking, and her lips had succeeded in finding one another and closing in a thin, controlled line. But the blazing blue eyes for which he loved her were fixed on him, a miracle of life in that pinched and narrow face. She could not trust herself to speak, but the eyes questioned, rejoiced, doubted and demanded, and, as so often, it was to the eyes alone that he spoke.

"I am quite sure of it," he said, watching her, giving her a little more time, for even sudden joy can come like a blow. "Everything is going to be all right. Put down your work, dear. When I was looking out of the window I saw something on the stream path coming down from the falls. Where Sylvie disappeared."

"Sylvia?" she asked thinly.

"Why, I should think so. No, don't get up. You can't see her now. She ought to be here any minute."

Before Ethel Fortier could answer, there came the sound of footsteps across the porch, the door opened, and Sylvia came in, shaking the moisture from her shoulders, her dark hair spangled with drops. Without greeting, she walked over to the fireplace and stood with her back to the low flames, facing her father and mother.

"Well," she said, a little defiantly, "I'm back."

Pete Fortier got up and went to stand beside his wife.

"That's good news on a rainy morning, isn't it?" he asked cheerfully, looking down at his wife rather than at the girl.

Ethel Fortier nodded and made a broken sound. Her body was trembling again, so that the crochet work she had been holding on her lap rolled off and fell to the floor unnoticed.

"Are you all right?" she asked at last.

Sylvia stood with eyes lowered, and so standing she had an almost sullen, shadowed look. The Indian strain, though actually weaker than in her father, was more apparent in her, in the wide cheekbones, the high nose, and the big shapely mouth. She was dark, too, whether naturally or through years of being in the sun it was impossible to tell, but there was color under the darkness, and the hair, which fell black and thick to her shoulders, hung in waving folds that moved with every motion of her head. Young as she was, there was power in her, power in the long-legged light body, power in the way she stood, motionless and guarded, power above all in the passive and unconquerable lines of her face.

Only when she raised her dark eyelids and looked at her parents did she show herself vulnerable. For her eyes were, like her mother's, blue, and where the dark immobility of her pose and face seemed an ageless inheritance, her eyes were intensely her own and young and unsure. They were not so bright as her mother's, but more the flowerlike blue of ice pools seen in April in some forest hollow.

"What do you mean by 'all right,' Mother?"

she asked. "You see I'm all here. I'm not starved or frozen or anything." And when her mother did not at once answer, she added, with an attempt at flippancy, "I've got all my feet and hands."

"There's some tea still in the tea pot, Sylvie," her father said in his carefully casual voice. "You'd better have yourself a cup."

But the girl did not seem to have heard.

"If you mean, am I the way I was when I left," she went on defiantly into her mother's silence, "I'm not."

Ethel Fortier's face went whiter, but she said almost hopefully, "Did you run off with Tom Ellison and get married in Millinocket, Sylvia? He's been wanting to marry you for a long while now."

"Tom Ellison?" repeated the girl. "No, it wasn't with Tom Ellison that I went, or with anyone like Tom Ellison."

Her mother started to rock violently back and forth in her rocking chair.

"For heaven's sake, Sylvia, who did you go off with? Are you married? Are you married, I say?"

Her husband laid his hand on her shoulder, until the chair was still again.

"There, there," he muttered. "What does it matter? The important thing is that we have Sylvie back again."

His wife looked at him with sudden hostility.

"You treat me like a child! You know where she's been and what she's been up to! You've had a queer look ever since she disappeared, like you'd seen a ghost. But you won't tell me! And she won't. Haven't I a right to know? Why should you two have secrets that I'm not to know? I'm her mother, aren't I? Who carried her and bore her, I'd like to know? Answer me, Sylvia. Are you married, have you a marriage certificate?"

Sylvia smiled, and in her slow smiling, insolence mingled with sweetness.

"I haven't got a certificate, Mother," she said. "But there *was* a marriage ceremony."

"With witnesses?"

"Heaps," and the girl smiled more broadly, looking off out of the window as though at some scene which no one else could see.

Her mother gave a kind of sob, partly of relief, partly of exasperation.

"Where is the man now?"

"I've left him."

"Left him? Did he let you go?"

"I went anyway."

"You should have stayed," said her father suddenly.

Sylvia turned to him.

"Why should I?" she demanded. "There are some things no girl can be expected to put up with. If I'd been a squaw it might have been different."

"My grandmother was a full-blooded Huron."

"Oh, I know that, Dad! But I'm Mother's child, too. I can't help being what I am, a mixture of both of you. When he came, I had to go with him, but afterwards I could no more have stayed than a spruce can grow above the timberline. I tried, really I tried, but I couldn't. I wanted to stay but I had to come away."

"You should have stayed," her father repeated.

"And gone on living in sin, Peter? You say that to your own daughter? Sometimes I feel as if you two were nothing but a pair of savages. I don't understand you. It comes of not being raised in a decent law-abiding town or going to church, either of you. I've tried and I've tried to bring Sylvia up right. I've read the Bible to her and done all I could to raise her decent, and

then she goes off with the first man who comes
by, and her own father says she should have
stayed with him."

Pete Fortier patted his wife's shoulder.

"Of course, Ethel," he said. "You've put up
with an awful lot all these years and been a good
wife and mother. Don't think about it any more.
Pretend it was a gale in the night, banging the
shutters and groaning the trees, and gone in the
morning. Let's all forget about it."

"Forget? She may have a child."

The girl at the fire stood up straighter, still
looking at what the others could not see.

"Probably I will."

"There! Listen to her! She's shameless, I say.
My father would have taken the strap to me and
turned me out of the house, if I'd come back
saying such things. But you stand there, Pete
Fortier, doing nothing!"

"Do you want me to take the strap to her,
Ethel?"

"Oh, you know I don't!" The woman began
to cry, then caught herself.

"What is his name, Sylvia?" she asked in a
hard voice.

The girl considered.

"Ola," she said, after a pause.

"Ola?" her mother caught it up. "Ola sounds like a Swede or a Norwegian. Was he from one of the logging camps? Oh, never mind. Keep your secrets, if you want to. I'll just have to do what I can, so it won't get out. I'll send a notice to the Millinocket paper, announcing Sylvia's marriage to Mr. Ola—what was his first name?"

The girl was smiling.

"It began with *P*." she said.

"Like your father's," Mrs. Fortier exclaimed. "What is the Swede for Peter? It isn't Pierre, of course. That's French, like some of your old friends still call you, Pete. But what's the Swede?"

"Per," said her husband.

"That's a funny-sounding name. We'll just say the wedding was from the house. Oh, I know that's a lie, but she did go *from* the house that morning—and then we'll say that she is now Mrs. P. Ola. No one will know the difference."

"And no one will care," said the girl. "No one but Mr. P. Ola."

"Well, that's all settled," exclaimed her father.

He had been watching Sylvia rather strangely. There was a brooding curiosity in that look, but no question, and no anxiety. His anxiety had been all for his wife, and now that he saw that she had at last groped her way to something tangible, by whose aid she could support the unknown, he left her and flung open the door, and the sweet chilly air came in and filled the hot room, and with it came the sound of the first white-throated sparrows singing and singing through the lightly falling rain.

For a minute Pete Fortier stood almost as immobile as Sylvia had stood, one broad shoulder leaning against the door frame, his face lifted a little to the suffused light and the gentle whispering sound. The last minutes had almost emptied him of strength, but he was resilient. Very soon, even before his wife could speak of the draught, he had turned back and, closing the door behind him, faced once more into the room.

"Go change your clothes, Sylvie," he said. "You're wet through. It seems good to have you back."

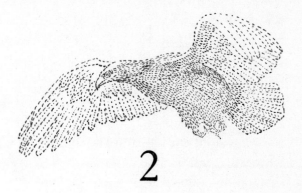

2

$\mathcal{E}$THEL FORTIER sighed and held up the finished work at arm's length to make sure that nothing had been left out. As a girl in Vermont she had learned to crochet, and twenty years of marriage to a forest ranger had turned her skill into an art. She fought back the green forest with two weapons, her crochet needles and her Bible, and when Pete Fortier found her engrossed in either, looking up at him when he spoke with bright blue eyes which scarcely saw him, he knew that she was wrestling once more with the angel of loneliness, and did everything within his power to help her in that stark struggle, where every victory could be only for a time and the vanquished would rise again like a strong man refreshed by sleep.

She had begun crocheting the great eagle on the afternoon of Sylvia's disappearance, leaving it to Pete to walk the woods which he loved, searching and calling among the rocks and glades, where only echoes answered him. That day there had been patches of snow still on the ground, the maple buds were just show-ing red, and the air smelled sweetly of wet earth coming back to life. At that moment of poise the black flies had not yet returned, but a robin was singing near the cabin. It had seemed part of the spring to have Sylvia back from the Millinocket high school for Easter vacation. Her mother had wanted to ask her many questions about life in the town, how her landlady and her family had been getting on, if the principal's wife had had her new baby yet, and whether she had been to church, but Sylvia had been very restless and gave only short answers. As usual, she had wanted to spend all her time out of doors, but instead of sunning herself as usual for quiet hours on the rocks by the edge of Katahdin Stream at the foot of the clearing, she was always on the move, exploring the woods or hurrying off to the beaver dam to watch the beavers, or helping her father to blaze a new trail around the foot of the mountain.

"Sylvia's different," Ethel Fortier had said to her husband. "She's growing up. She needs more young company. We must ask Tom Ellison for supper some day soon, and perhaps he can bring some boys along, if he has anyone down at the camp helping him to get ready for summer."

"Don't worry about Sylvie," Pete Fortier said. "She can come to no harm. She knows the woods as well as I do. I've told her not to go above the timberline. With so much ice on the trails, a person could come to trouble up there."

"You've never been up to the summit yourself, have you, Pete?" Ethel asked. It had always seemed strange to her that Pete never wanted to climb Katahdin. A hundred times she had heard him asked to go with some party, and every time he had made some excuse. Sometimes he had laughed and said that he had no head for heights, but she knew that this was all nonsense. If the reason had been a physical one, he would have set about overcoming the handicap at once. It was probably one of his superstitions. While he had left his religion with his childhood, he had brought his superstitions with him, French-Canadian superstitions, deepened with Indian, against which Ethel's common sense and Methodism had battled in vain. The truth was that she found them attractive. They were endearing in him, and roused in her an inconsequential tenderness. It was because he was so different from the boys of Montpelier with whom she had grown up that she had loved Pete Fortier from the first time she had met him at the Millinocket hotel where she, a young teacher, was staying until she had decided on a boarding house. Brought up in the intimacies and rigidities of a decent small-town household, she had married him at the end of the term and followed him into the daunting loneliness of the wilderness, which for her had always remained truly a wilderness.

Of what that wilderness meant to Pete, Ethel had little idea. He was very often alone in the woods for hours and days, and at these times he was aware of other presences which shared the springs and trails with him. He often sensed someone a little ahead of him whom he could never overtake, and even oftener turned his head to catch a glimpse of someone who followed, always out of sight.

"The Indians are still here," he thought, and being part Indian himself, he found the idea not unpleasant.

And there were later presences of whom he was also aware as he followed fifty-year-old tote roads so overgrown that only a woodsman's eye could have traced them at all. He did not feel so close to the loggers as he did to the Indians, although the traces of their occupancy of the forest were much more marked; for the destruction of their hands stood all about him in the pine stumps, often six or seven feet across, blackened and eaten out by old fires into curious shapes, which crouched and menaced from the underbrush.

Once, on a late afternoon of coming storm, Pete had followed the scarred blazes of a forgotten trail and had suddenly arrived at a long-deserted camp, its windows broken out, the last of the door hanging askew and seventeen axes lying scattered on the floor.

The rain began almost at once and Pete sought shelter, but the way the seventeen axe-heads blazed up at him in every flare of the lightning, and the door banged on crying hinges, and something moved in the darkness at the end of the building, soon drove him out into the the storm again.

A third presence, more dominant than those of either Indians or loggers, was always with Pete when he was alone in the woods. As his grand-mother's people had done, he interpreted the tranquillity of some days, the cold restlessness of others, and the sudden violent storms that swept the forests, as the moods of the mountain itself. Once he and another man had been in a canoe on one of the ponds, when his companion made some careless joke about the spirit who ruled the heights of Katahdin. A moment later they heard a sound behind them and looking back towards the quiet cove they had just left, saw a waterspout form in a whirling column, towering high above their heads into the blue sky, and of such force that it could easily

32

have lifted the canoe into the air. But the spout did not follow them; it dissolved as suddenly as it had formed, filling the air with falling water and spray.

From that day, Pete Fortier never mentioned the spirit's name. He minded his own business and kept to the forest lands, going no farther up the slope than the spruces dare to climb. And in his own realm he felt at peace with all the unseen forces of the woods.

Tom Ellison had accepted that invitation to supper, but he had never come, because the day before he was due Sylvia disappeared. One moment she was distractedly going off, leaving her bed unmade, and letting the door slam behind her, and the next moment she had disappeared without a word or a sign of any sort, except for her red hair-ribbon, which her father found just before dusk on the rock ledge at the foot of Katahdin Falls. He had brought the ribbon back to Ethel, but he had not told her that it had been lying on the stone in the shape of a heart, weighted down with smooth pebbles.

All that first night he had hunted for her and

worn out two batteries in his electric torch. Once he had come on Sylvie's footprints in a patch of snow. For a tall girl, she had very small feet. Even in his worry and exhaustion he had felt proud of the neat, sure track she had left behind her. There were the prints of other feet alongside hers. Pete looked at them, too, for a long time. Then he trampled them all out and went home.

It was almost dawn. He had found Ethel sitting up fully dressed, and her crocheted eagle was well begun. During the next days it grew quickly, fierce turned head, wings with a two-foot spread, claws which gripped the rock. In the pattern, the eagle held two crossed flags, but Ethel had changed the design to suit her, as she often did. The room was hung with her crocheted pictures in natural wood frames which Pete had become skillful in making. The eagle was to hang over the mantel.

Although Ethel had worked every spare minute since Sylvia's return, the devil of solitude had not been downed. Even while Pete was removing a now discarded picture of two kittens from the place of honor and temporarily tack-

34

ing up the eagle in its place with thumbtacks, she was already reaching for her second and final resource, the Bible, lying close to the lamp on the table at her side. It opened of itself to Revelations. For her the beasts of the Apocalypse were very real, much more real than the moose or deer or bear which had so long been her neighbors and which interested her very little as such. Man-headed, animal-bodied, monstrous, her visionary animals reared up from the clouds, their great shoulders shutting out the stars. It was their cries which she sometimes heard at night from the darkness of the forest. They were to her a terror and a consolation, foretelling the end of the world, which sometimes seemed to her very near and not unwelcome.

Sylvia also was sitting by the light of the same lamp, but she was reading an old magazine impatiently, fingering the pages and bending their corners.

Suddenly she let the wide pages fall.

"Let's go canoeing, Dad!" she exclaimed. "The moon will soon be up. It's full tonight."

"Don't you have some school work to do before you go back Sunday?" her mother asked.

"School work?" Sylvia repeated. "I'm not going back. Did you think I was going back?"

Her mother tightened her lips, her eyes still on the page before her.

"I think you ought to graduate," she said. "I've sent a notice to the paper that your husband's gone to Vermont as foreman of a lumber camp, but that you are planning to finish your education before joining him."

"Mother, you can tell any stories you like to the papers, if it makes you feel better, but I can't and won't go back. School? Why, I might as well go back to a skipping-rope and dolls."

"It's a nice evening," Pete joined in. "The wind's swung into the west. If you don't mind being alone, Ethel, we might go out on Daicey to watch the moon rise. We'll be back soon."

After twenty years, he still asked her consent before leaving her unnecessarily, but he knew that she was never afraid to be alone. The attack which she withstood was not a physical one.

Sylvia walked ahead down the trail by the edge of the stream. After so much rain the ground was spongy under their feet, but they made their way easily by starlight, stepping over the faint darkness of roots and the faint pallor of stones, while the stream beside them outran them, whispering and singing in its rocky channel.

At the head of the lake Pete kept a canoe under a low shelter, inconspicuous among the bushes. Father and daughter had so often worked and played together that no word was needed between them as they lifted it from the crossbars where it rested, carried it down to the pond, and slid it into the dark cold water. Already the east was brightening with the coming of the not-yet-risen moon, and as they paddled out into the middle of the pond, suddenly, like a specter, Katahdin appeared against the sky, rising above the countless trees that before had hidden it. The rains had washed the granite slopes bare, but still the crevices were white with the winter's snow, and on this the light of the unseen moon shone and glittered coldly. To the west there were clouds, dark humped shapes, part of the shadows that touched everything but the heights of that one high mountain, dressed in brightness.

Pete and Sylvia floated, watching the light

spread lower and lower down the slopes, and at last the moon rose and made a slatted and shining path in which they moved.

There seemed to be no wind, but small ripples crinkled against the sides of the canoe, making a repeated sound, so small that the ear noticed it only as a soothing echo of the far-off sound of the waterfall. An owl hooted and its mate answered it. The next time they called, they had moved, still bound to one another by the cord of their answering cries. High up in heaven there must have been some wind, for the clouds were moving up the sky from the west, and as the two in the canoe watched, first one constellation and then another was erased from the dark board of the sky.

"What you did is dangerous." Pete Fortier's voice came from the stern of the canoe.

Sylvia did not turn her head.

"I know," she said. For a moment it seemed as though she were about to say more, but then she sighed, and repeated, "I know."

Again there was silence except for the faint calling of the waters and the occasional cries of the owls.

Suddenly a brazen light flushed all the cloud bank and was gone, then came another and another. There was no thunder, only the pulsing red light in the west while in the east the full moon stood, spreading an icy greenness over all she saw.

Silently, with two or three long thrusts of his paddle, Pete Fortier turned the canoe and headed for the shore. Sylvia caught the stroke, and they shot forward, like some great water bird either in pursuit or flight. But over their heads the elements moved faster still. Now from the mounting clouds the lightning flashed in blinding rivers, like thin cataracts of destruction, and the crash of thunder followed like the downfall of high towers of brass. The wind sprang on the trees, so that they thrashed their branches and roared, and the pond was white with snapping waves that threw themselves against the bow of the boat, which still pushed on. Now the whole dome of the sky was covered with rushing clouds from which broke sheets of lightning and the torn terror of the thunder. Katahdin's crest was darkened, but still in the east the moon shone from a cloudless sky and cast a serene pallor across her half of the world.

The canoe grated on shingle, and father and daughter leaped out into the cold shallow water, which seemed to strike at them.

Such was the hold of training that they each caught a thwart and heaved the light craft up on the shore, but then Pete dropped his hold and pushed his daughter towards the path to the cabin. They moved along a way lighted by torches of lightning. Now came the rain, in great gouts beating upon them as though they were passing under the arrowed folds of a waterfall. Through it shook the lightning. The simultaneous thunder half deafened them.

"Faster!" yelled Pete between roars, but either the girl could not or would not go faster. The lightning was striking about them now. They could hear its hiss and crack like the hiss and crack of an enormous whip, and then came the splintering outcry of a stricken tree. He pushed past her and catching one of her hands broke into a run, but she pulled herself free and stopped.

Pete came back and shouted in her ear, "The cabin! Quick!"

Through all the confusion of sound, he heard her say clearly, "No need to bring Mother into this."

Then a little later, when he could again hear her, she said, "Get me a slicker, Dad, I've sprained my ankle, I think."

The lightning blazed beside them, and a maple tree, not twenty feet away, split open, one half falling slowly, its small vibrant leaves in the next flash of light showing stiff and bright as leaves of metal.

Pete glared at his daughter. Her hair hung close to her head like a black veil molded to a skull, her eyes blazed into his, and she was smiling. Then came the darkness and then the light. Another tree on the other side of them gave its death cry, as he sat down on a boulder. She stood facing him streaming with rain, smiling the same curious, almost amused smile. He was sure her ankle was not hurt. For some reason she was anxious to get him away from her own proximity. But he would not budge. Intent on his own plans, he knelt down on the wet leaves and when she saw what he was trying to do, she helped him as she could, holding her sweater over the little pile of tobacco he was making from crumbled cigarettes and laying on a stone. The cigarette lighter raised its little flame bravely in the heart of the storm.

Another tree near them was ripped half naked of bark, a white birch lurched and fell sideways, the loud cataract of rain never stopped. But Pete Fortier succeeded after many failures in lighting the little heap of tobacco, and his Sylvia tended and sheltered the flame, and slowly into the saturated air rose the strong smoke, blown sideways, flattened almost to the ground, but still filtering upwards, mingling its alien odor with all the smells of earth and moss and leaves rising from the beaten earth.

When the storm at last roared down the Sourdnahunk and the valley, Sylvia and her father went back to the cabin, and he saw, as he had expected to see, that she walked as lightly as ever.

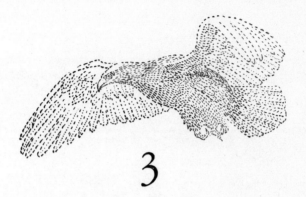

3

$\mathcal{T}$HAT SUMMER there were many people on the mountain. The camps were filled; parties of men, women, and children dotted the trails, and the more adventurous followed paths of their own making. Pete was busy from morning to night. He answered questions, distributed maps, listened for forbidden shots, hunted for lost campers, and in general guarded and enforced the law through his share of the wilderness. Now for Ethel Fortier came the days of plenty, when she was never lonely, when there were many

45

faces and voices, new and old, when for every
meal she set the table for guests, never knowing
who or how many they might be. Her face became fuller and fresher, like a wilted flower that
has been put in a glass of clear water. Neglected
lay her crochet needles, and at night she no
longer looked out into the darkness, longing
above all things to see the lighted windows of a
neighbor's house. Even the Bible was seldom
opened, or if she read at all she read the Psalms
of Thanksgiving.

*He sendeth the springs into the valleys,
which run among the hills.*

*They give drink to every beast of the field;
the wild asses quench their thirst.*

*By them shall the fowls of the heaven have
their habitation, which sing among the
branches.*

He watereth the hills. . . .

*Praise ye him, sun and moon: praise him,
all ye stars of light.*

*Praise him, ye heavens of heavens, and ye
waters that be above the heavens. . . .*

*Praise the Lord from the earth, ye dragons,
and all deeps:*

46

*Fire, and hail; snow, and vapours; stormy
wind fulfilling his word:
Mountains . . . .*

Certainly she felt herself a part of the rhythms
of the year. She came into bloom as annually as
the cosmos in her small garden. She forgot the
loneliness, which had retreated from her as
surely as the snows had retreated from the
heights of Katahdin. Now Pete heard again her
unexpectedly warm, pretty laugh, which, like
her eyes, seemed to belong to a different person
imprisoned in her rigid flesh. He could relax
the constant care with which he guarded her at
other times. For three months she could take
care of herself.

About Sylvia he felt none of the usual anxie-
ties, though he believed that danger of another
sort still threatened her. But in her relations to
people she had matured. She was very seldom
irritable with her mother any more, and with
outsiders her manner was pleasant and casual.
Even her walk had gained a new assurance. In
the old days she had seemed to be searching for
something, not knowing what it was. Now she

appeared, to her father at least, to be following a trail to an end she knew of.

Tom Ellison, who ran the big camp on a nearby pond, as his parents had run it before him, continued to come up to the ranger's cabin as often as he could get away. Sylvia welcomed him as she welcomed any other visitor. He was a pleasant-looking young man, blond, with straight nose, good features, and a skin that flushed easily in a boyish way. All this would have been misleading to anyone who did not read the rather cold determination in his gray eyes. Ethel Fortier truly loved him. He was everything which she thought it desirable for a young man to be: well bred, well raised, well educated, and doing well. Of course he knew about Sylvia's marriage. One of his names for her was Mrs. O., but the knowledge had in no way cooled his interest in her. It seemed almost to have increased it, as though he realized that he had once made the mistake of waiting too long, and would not again err in that direction.

One day he took her to see something which even her father did not know about. He had blazed a trail to the spot, but when they were half-way there, he lost his way and climbed to the top of a spruce to spy out the land, while she waited below.

"We're headed all right," he said when he came down.

"What is it, Tom?" she asked. But he wouldn't tell her. A little farther on, they came to a well-marked game trail. Tom was leading the way, on his shoulders a light pack that held an axe, a small coffee pot, and the lunch she had put up for them. It was so warm that they had brought no sweaters, and moved along easily, dressed almost alike in shirts and shorts, wool socks and boots. Even in the uniform of their youth, they looked like allegorical figures, Day followed by Night.

They had been walking in silence, she well behind him, so that the branches would not slap back into her face after his passing. Suddenly he stopped and stepped aside for her to come up beside him, which she did, too wise in the ways of the woods to make any sound. Looking eagerly through the trees, she saw an opening about twenty feet across with a surface of trampled clay and water. In every direction game trails led into it, like the spokes of a wheel, and at the hub three deer were standing, unaware of being watched.

In those endless miles of moss-floored forest, the place was an interlude. Every inch of it was pocked with hoof marks, and several birds perched on the stones, bending their heads to peck at the clay beneath them. Sylvia turned smiling to her companion and nodded. Then she clapped her hands, and when the birds flew up and the deer bounded off, the white flags of their tails flying high, she laughed aloud.

"What a wonderful place this is," she said, finding a fallen tree to sit on. "What is it? A salt lick?"

"I think it must be. I suppose there was a pond here once. All kinds of animals come. I saw a bobcat here the day I found it."

"And now you and I have come," said Sylvia idly.

He sat down beside her and repeated her words.

"Yes, you and I have come. I have been wanting to talk with you, Sylvie, where we wouldn't be interrupted."

She did not look at him. Her eyes were on the sky over the glade where two eagles were circling, one clockwise and the other counter-clockwise, almost as though they moved in some aerial ritual dance. He could not be sure she had heard him, but he went on.

"About this marriage, Sylvie. Are you really married?"

"Enough so that I am going to have a baby," she answered, without turning her eyes from the eagles, which were now circling directly above them as though they had found what they were looking for.

Tom Ellison was not taken aback by her answer.

"I thought so," he said. "I don't know what has happened and I don't want to know. You needn't ever talk about it. But I love you, Sylvie. I always have, even when you were a little girl in pigtails. I waited too long to say so. I thought after you were through school would be time enough—but I waited too long. Now I want to marry you. Then you'll have a husband when the baby's born. I swear to you that I will treat it always as though it were mine."

51

He waited for her to answer, but she only said, "Look! The eagles have found us! They are watching."

"Sylvie," he said, and she pulled her eyes from the eagles.

"You're good to me, Tom, much too good. Thank you. But I can't."

"Why not?"

"I'm married already."

"I don't believe it for a minute! No husband would go off and leave a girl like you, Sylvie."

"I left him."

"So much the worse for him, then! Do you mean to go back?"

"No."

"What do you mean to do, Sylvie?"

"Just stay here and when the baby comes, take care of it."

"Without a father?"

"Without a father."

"But, Sylvie, you can't do that. No one will believe that you're married. Everyone will talk, Sylvie."

"Let them talk."

"I don't ask you to love me. I don't even ask

you to live with me until you're ready to. But
I want to be your husband, to look out for you,
to stand by you when the baby comes."

She laughed.

"You want to knock down anyone who says
I'm no better than I should be, Tom. I do ap-
preciate it, but I can't."

And all his arguments, all his entreaties could
get no other answer from her. When at last he
gave up, she laid her brown hand lightly on his.

"I don't know much about religion," she said,
"but I do think that we should reap as we sow. I
have to go through this as it was begun. I'm all
right, Tom. You don't have to feel sorry for me."

"You don't understand!" he cried again. "I
love you."

"And I love him. You don't understand that,
either."

Afterwards, they talked about other things
and later he built a fire at the edge of the clay
and made coffee and they ate their sandwiches.

Only once did he look at the eagles. "What
the devil do they keep circling us for?" he demanded, with sudden anger. "If I had a gun, I'd
teach them to mind their own business."

"And then Dad would have to mind *his* business and give you a summons," Sylvia said without smiling.

He didn't answer, and after a moment he heard her add, as though to herself, "Perhaps they *are* minding their own business."

"I don't know what you mean by that remark," he broke in with rare irritation, for though he was a man not at all averse to using his fists, he almost always spoke pleasantly, having been brought up under the disciplines of a position in which the guest is always in the right. But she only smiled at him and bit into her sandwich, and from that time on they spoke and acted like any two young acquaintances picnicking at the foot of a mountain.

Summer passed slowly and autumn came. The swamp maples first caught the message, the boughs of the popples turned yellow, the bark of the white birch reflected the lemon of changing leaves. Now at night the northern lights flamed behind the high crest of Katahdin and the loons called through the darkness, getting ready for their long flight. The camps were no longer crowded; the trails were almost empty of hikers. Pete Fortier could breathe again, and his wife, Ethel, treasured the rare visit of anyone who stopped at the cabin. The time of loneliness lay before her, and one evening, after two days of rain, Pete raised his head from his book to the faint familiar click of crochet needles and knew that for him the time of watchfulness had come again.

This year life presented unusual problems. It was perfectly clear to anyone that Sylvia was pregnant. She had taken on a new beauty, and went about, dignified and brooding, asking nothing. The bond between father and daughter held, strong as ever, but she did not confide in him. After nearly thirty years in the service, Pete knew something of cabin fever. Two can live out a winter shut in together; four, too, can weather the months and remain friends. But not three. Slowly, inevitably, two find themselves taking sides against the third. Even though the pattern might shift—two parents against the child, two women against the man, two outdoor people against the indoor woman —in time one or other of the tensions would become dominant, and when spring opened the windows and doors to the world, the three would be ruined as a family.

This Pete Fortier was determined to prevent. He took the opportunity of Sylvia's presence to make many trips to the outlying frontiers of his district, often being gone for four or five days at a time. Then he fairly forced Sylvia into a fortnight's visit with a friend in Millinocket, and when she came back, he kept at Ethel until, leaving her crochet work behind, she went off to Montpelier, a thing she ordinarily refused to do, as she did not consider it part of a wife's duty to leave her husband to care for himself.

She had been back for only a few days when the baby was born. There were eight inches of snow, and the doctor had to come by plane. By the time he reached the cabin the baby had been bathed and dressed and was asleep in her basket. However, he looked mother and child over, complimented Ethel on what he found, made out the birth certificate, shook hands several times with Pete, and disappeared as he had come.

It was only after the doctor was gone that Pete trusted himself to look at the baby. It seemed like any other he had seen—red, knotted-up, frowning and determined, as though it had just fought its way into life and the air, as indeed it had.

"What a miracle," he thought. "This morning you were living like a fish, and now here you are on land." Whatever he had expected he might see, this baby girl was like any other baby girl.

"She's a beautiful child," said Ethel, slipping her veined hand into the crook of his arm. "She's prettier even than Sylvia was."

Pete laughed.

"It takes a woman to think they're pretty at this age," he said. "Is Sylvie really pleased it's a girl? What is she going to call her?"

Ethel smiled, her beautiful incongruous eyes flashing with a rare look of mischief.

"Oh, she's your daughter, Pete," she said tolerantly. "She really is delighted to have a girl, just as you were, and she's giving her another of your fancy Frenchified names. As though there weren't enough good names in the world, like Barbara and Alice and Catherine! But she won't listen, any more than you listened to me when she was born."

"She's calling her Sylvia?" he asked.

"No, not Sylvia. She says she's going to name her Claire."

"Claire," Pete repeated, evidently pleased. And he began to hum the most often sung of all the old voyageur songs, *"À la claire fontaine."*

4

$\mathcal{F}$ROM THE FIRST, Ethel Fortier loved the baby. She was so absorbed in this new life that she no longer wondered what people thought about Sylvia; and, perhaps as never before, the weight of solitude was lifted from her shoulders. Pete was often away on his rounds, and when she could, Sylvia went with him, trekking long miles through the woods on her snowshoes after her father, eating sparely in the shelter of a rock, reading the life and death of their forest neighbors written on the snow. But Ethel, who had been Ethel Townsend, daughter of Lawyer John Q. A. Townsend of Montpelier, stayed at home, an alien in the woods as she had been from the first, but for the first time almost reconciled, now that there were three generations under the cabin roof, a nucleus of human life unfolding in the wilderness.

That winter a great deal of snow fell, without much wind; the branches drooped under their mounded loads, and seen from the open, Katahdin blazed like a vast fragment of fallen star. Between white banks, Katahdin Stream poured, black and strange, a stream of onyx, whose spray froze into crystal. In the clear air of winter, the crash and uproar of the falls carried a long distance, but the weighted snow silenced the murmur of the branches, so that now the stream sang alone.

Sylvia was rather quiet that winter. Her father often saw her looking thoughtfully at Claire. She had a natural gift for handling the baby, and her eyes were tender as she bathed and dressed her, but her love had a certain watchful reticence about it, which he thought he understood.

It was Ethel, rather than Sylvia, who talked about Claire when Tom tramped up from the pond to see them, a frequent visitor whom the baby very early seemed to recognize. She would crow with pleasure when he picked her up, and laugh and kick to be tossed in his arms, showing a complete fearlessness, and happiest when tossed the highest.

"Look out, Tom! You'll drop her!" Ethel Fortier would cry, clasping her hands anxiously, but beaming upon them both, while Sylvia watched in silence. A stranger would certainly have supposed at such times that he had come upon a complete family, and his first impression would have been that the grandmother and the blond young father loved the baby most, for the other two showed little of their feelings.

As Claire grew older, her hair became dark as her mother's but without the waving tendrils that had covered Sylvia's head at her age. Her baby blue eyes changed into gray, very large and clear. Like her mother's and grandmother's, her eyes were beautiful, but their expression varied to an unusual degree. At most times they were dark and a little flecked like granite, but

63

when Tom Ellison played with her, making her leap and laugh, they shone very bright and seemed lighter, and in her rages, they were almost black.

For very early Claire showed a capacity for extraordinary outbursts of temper. One moment she would be smiling and playing with her fingers, and the next moment some discomfort or hunger would set her to howling in black fury, beating her fists and raging until she lost her breath and turned purple in the face. Unless the discomfort passed, or she had her way, she would not stop, however exhausted she might become. It was strange and daunting to see such a capacity for fury in so small and soft a being, and it affected her family in different ways.

Ethel gave in to the baby always, Pete took down his snowshoes and went out, but Sylvia stiffened her own will and tried to teach Claire that such outbursts would get her nowhere. As for Tom, if he happened to be present, he broke into laughter, and snatching the baby out of her crib, would toss her far above his head, catching her again and again at the last possible moment, until her screams changed into wild shrieks of delight.

In early March, there came a spell of warm days, and close to the earth the snow began to melt. Katahdin Stream was swollen with icy water, and the bluejays began to give their sonorous wood-wind calls of love from the budding tops of the trees. Sylvia no longer went out with her father, but wandered off alone, and her mother guessed when she came back that she had been crying.

The bright blue days were followed by days of rain. The branches soughed, the falls cried and exulted, and the pussywillow buds shone on the slender reddening twigs.

Then one evening the clouds began to open and the sun went down in fire behind the black slopes of Katahdin. There was a feeling in the air that afternoon which made Pete Fortier uneasy. He happened to be far from home, investigating a rumor of illegal trapping, but he turned back earlier than usual, filled with a sense of impending disaster.

As Ethel knew, Pete was superstitious, and when he received these inner warnings he heeded them, feeling that they might come from sources which it was wise to obey. That day he pushed himself to get home. The wet snow was bad for traveling and he was tired. Whenever possible he followed his old trail, where the packed snowshoe track stood up firm and clear-cut above the shrinking surface. Everywhere else the rotten snow lay dull and dirty gray, and the ice at the edge of the streams was honey-combed and made a tinkling sound when the water stirred it. Several times he passed deer tracks and once some moose had gone by recently. They must be leaving the yards where they had sheltered all winter. The birds were uttering cries of alarm, and as he drew nearer the cabin, he was sorry to see the pair of eagles again quartering the sky over its roof as they had done all the previous autumn. This was the first time he had seen them this year, and he would rather that they had not been there.

When he reached the cabin, everything seemed all right. Perhaps Sylvia was whiter than usual, and he thought that her eyes looked a little swollen from crying. The baby was asleep; Ethel was setting the table for supper. The red sunset was dying away into ashes, and he had just started to light the big oil lamp when there came a groan from the mountain.

Pete knew the sound, although he had heard

it only once before and then at a great distance. This time it was different. It came from their side of the slope, high up, where on some granite ledge the snow, melted along the rock, had begun to slide with a rasping of boulders and then the creaking and crashing of trees. Pete blew out the lamp he was lighting and put it down with a steady hand.

"Get into your coats," he told the women. "Quick. Tie something over your heads. Sylvie, you take Claire. Where's my axe? Thanks, Sylvie. Have you both your mittens? Fill your pockets with bread. Anything. We may have to dig our way out. Ethel, help me move the furniture. If the house turns over we may still be able to get out through the windows. It's strong. It might hold."

Ethel did not cry out now against the coming end. She helped move tables and heavy chairs into the bedrooms and then came and stood close to her husband by the wall with his arm about her. Sylvia, holding Claire, wedged herself into the corner near them.

"What about the stove, Dad?" she asked. "If the house turns over?"

There was a pail by the sink, and he lifted a

stove lid and threw the water in, filling the room with hissing steam. The shrieks and groans above them were gathering volume and speed. The sound was both loud and muffled at the same time. And now they could see in the twilight a moving whiteness pouring down upon them. Trees were swallowed up into it. Spruce, hemlocks, maples, and popples—they all made no resistance. Twenty feet high, the wall of snow, bristling with the torn forest, grumbling with great boulders, roared down upon them. Now it had reached the flats below the falls and still it came on. Pete felt Sylvia move from beside him. With quick sure steps she ran towards the windows that faced the avalanche and held Claire up in her mittened hands.

"Look at that, Baby!" he heard her cry. "See the pretty snow!"

Her voice, young and defiant, pierced through the voice of the avalanche. And then he knew that the latter was weakening. It no longer shook the air. The slide was moving more and more slowly. After all, the flats had been wide enough! Not a hundred feet from the cabin, the wall of snow came groaning to a halt. In the twilight, its

68

whiteness reared high above them, threatening them like another mountain, and all that spring the cabin stood in a stream of water, flowing from its slow disintegration, so that day and night they lived in a continual lisping and trickling of melting snow.

5

$\mathcal{D}$URING THE next five years, Pete Fortier noticed many things. For one, there were great numbers of forest fires, and these usually occurred in the spring rather than in the fall, when they would have seemed more natural. For another thing, the majority were on their side of the mountain, and were apparently set by lightning bolts rather than by the carelessness of campers. Some of these fires were very small and easily checked. Others raged for days in combs of fire and smoke, roaring and ravening

73

down the slopes, towards the cabin. Pete became very wary, and during the spring months his eye scanned every horizon for smoke and his nostrils tested every breeze for its taint.

For another thing, the wild animals in his district seemed to be greatly on the increase. At night the raccoons would come. Sometimes at early twilight, sometimes in the middle of the night when the moon was high overhead, or again in the first pallor of dawn, there would be a loud clatter and bang from near the back door, and in the morning Ethel would find the garbage pail rolled over and spilling its contents.

There had never been such an incursion of woodmice in the cabin. The presence of Ethel's cat did little to stem the tide, and in vain Pete stopped up mouseholes, for new ones appeared as quickly as old ones were plugged. The mice were everywhere. Ethel hated to reach up to any high shelf for fear of finding a mouse under her fingers. The incursion bore most heavily on her. Claire liked it, and fed the little creatures secretly, coaxing them into her lap. Sylvia ignored them, Pete's objections were practical, but Ethel became increasingly nervous and would wake up with a scream when they ran across her bed at night.

The wear and fret of the mice was increased by the wasps, which insisted upon building over the screen door, and by the plague of flies, which on certain days were sucked down the chimney to scatter in buzzing clots all over the cabin.

And as if these small continual incursions were not enough, the moose chose to make a new trail close to the corner of the cabin. At any moment of the day or night a great crackling and crashing was likely to be heard, and their snorts and bellowings held for Ethel an Apocalyptic terror.

Deer, too, were everywhere, and porcupines destroyed more trees than Pete could remember, but it was in the predatory creatures that the increase was most marked. The hawks and owls seemed much more numerous. Their callings sounded by day and by night, and he seldom looked up without seeing the eagles, which seemed to spy out all their goings and comings. Several times he almost walked into a bear at the turn of a trail and invariably the creature stood its ground with sleepy insolence. The bobcats were about in unusual numbers. Pete frequently came upon a recent kill of theirs, and he had found larger tracks which made him believe that there were lynxes in the neighborhood, nor did he speak to anyone of the wolves he had seen trotting across the open ridges, where no wolf had trotted for a hundred years.

He mentioned these matters in his official reports, but without emphasis, and more as possibilities than as established facts. But none of the other rangers had noticed any marked changes in their districts, as he discovered upon discreet questioning.

One evening in March, Sylvia, hearing someone on the porch, opened the door, expecting to see Tom, but instead found herself facing a big bobcat crouched in the lamplight as though about to spring. The sudden light, fortunately, dazzled him and she slammed the door in his face.

They saw the vixen first on a night when the moon kept appearing between black clouds like a rolling eyeball. The creature stood prick-eared at the back of the cabin, not ten feet from the door, yapping and dark against the rotten snow.

Every evening she came back to yap some more. She seemed perfectly unafraid of people, and only moved back a little when Pete went out, slapping his hands together to drive her away. Only when he shot over her head did she finally leave, and then she was back the next night, and sat in the rain, her sharp barks piercing the quiet drip-drop of the shower.

But one day Sylvia came upon her body in the trail, torn and disembowelled, and Pete said that a bobcat must have got her.

"Do you suppose she had young ones?" Sylvia asked, and her father nodded.

"I'm afraid so."

It took him four days to find the den, and then there was only one of the litter left alive. He brought it back on his arm, a little vixen, red and bedraggled, with a sharp nose and whiskers like threads of silk, and so light and thin that she seemed only a rag of fur. From the first, Claire was devoted to the little fox. She was gentleness itself with the newcomer. She learned to feed it warm milk, first from a dropper and later from a baby's bottle, and her elders were surprised to find how sure and light her hands could be.

Vixie she called the little fox at first, and then Vicki. From the beginning Ethel's big cream-colored cat was friendly, and allowed the little fox to sleep with him behind the stove. When on the second day Ethel saw him hold Vicki between his long yellow arms and wash her thoroughly, she smiled and said, "The little fox will be all right now. What a young animal needs is to be washed and washed. Otherwise they never seem to thrive."

Now Vicki throve, and by the next spring was full grown, larger than most foxes, with a bright coat, and very tame towards those whom she knew.

By the time Claire was five years old, Ethel Fortier's earlier devotion had changed into an almost unbroken irritation. And yet the child was so beautiful, and could be so engaging, that at times the grandmother's heart still went soft with pride and affection. Claire was never more beautiful than in her rages. Then her eyes stood black and enormous in her face, sparkling with unshed tears of fury; her skin turned a transparent white; and her heavy hair seemed to lift on her forehead like a pine bough lifted by a wind. Almost anything could bring on these spells of rage, but sometimes days passed without a sign of them and she went about humming and murmuring to herself almost as constantly as Katahdin Stream.

She had indeed a passion for running water. As soon as she could drag a chair to the sink, she learned to climb up to dabble in the pail of water standing there, and when someone pulled her away, she went into one of her furies. Even as a very small girl, unable to walk, she would sit very still, listening to the sound of the waterfall coming through the open window, and later her every expedition led her to the edge of the stream. Because of this, Pete had fenced in a yard in front of the house with a sign "Shut the Gate" at the entrance and an intricate lock, so that when she slipped out of the house Claire would still be caged away from the dangerous magnet that drew her.

One Saturday after dinner Pete started off on his rounds. Tom was expected up from the camp. The summer before, he had been very much in love with a girl from Pittsburgh who was staying at the camp for two weeks. She had extended her holiday to a month, and they had been together from morning till night, but later, after she returned home, she wrote him that she was marrying the man to whom she had been engaged all along.

As Pete Fortier stood by the door, looking about him with animal caution and animal awareness, his eyes took in the scene, which never seemed commonplace to him though he had seen it thousands of times. Overhead the sky was cloudy, but even as he watched, the wind opened blue casement upon blue casement. The swallows were weaving their mazes above the stream, the light flashing on their white bellies and sleek blue-bottle backs. Nearby a robin was drinking from a little rill flowing from a last snowbank, and having drunk, it forded the streamlet and ran along a bare patch of old grass, stopping and cocking its head to listen for the faint talk of worms beneath the ground. When it ran it put one foot in front of the other, Indian fashion, but when it hopped, its feet were almost side by side, with the left a little ahead.

Only Katahdin Peak was wrapped in black

impenetrable cloud and took no part in the lightening of the day.

Pete put his head inside the door.

"There's a storm on the mountain," he said to Sylvia. "Don't take a long hike with Claire."

She nodded, looking up from the book she was reading, and Pete went over to his wife to kiss her goodbye. Ethel was sitting in the straight-backed chair beside the radio ready for the opera. She was wearing her silk dress and earrings and her buckled slippers, and she returned his kiss rather primly, as though they were in a public place. As he went out he heard the first notes of *Carmen,* rather faint and scratchy, and thought to himself that he must get new batteries for the old radio. On his way to the trail, he looked to see how the fiddleneck ferns in the hollow were coming on. Ethel liked them for spring greens, and he was glad to see their curled tops showing strongly. Then, glancing at his watch, he made off, careful to shut the gate behind him.

When Tom arrived for the afternoon, he, too, carefully shut the gate. But an hour later, while Ethel listened to *Carmen,* and Sylvia and

Tom played double canfield, Claire got it open. She had been studying the gate for a long time, trying this thing and that, and now at last she opened it into freedom, and with Vicki at her side entered into her heritage.

It was some time later that Tom said, "Doesn't that darned fox ever stop yapping?"

Sylvia, who had been so absorbed that she had not even heard the radio ten feet away, now raised her head, startled, then bounded from her seat, upsetting the card table, and ran out of the door like a spirit. She saw that the gate was open, and heard the fox barking down by the stream. But what had happened? The stream had doubled. Running with her hair and dress whipping back, she reached the new bank. The water was roaring down from the mountain. There had been a cloudburst above, and Claire, playing by the bank, had been caught in the flash flood. Nothing could live in that rush. But Vicki was still yapping by the uptorn roots of an old pine which had gone over in a long-ago blow and which, usually well above the bank, now stretched out into the swirling water.

Then Sylvia saw the pale something wedged

among the dead branches. Without hesitation she pulled herself onto the trunk and ran along it. After the first few steps, the water rushed over her feet and then her ankles. The force was terrific, and suddenly she felt herself being torn away from her footing as though strong hands were plucking her off. Throwing herself forward, she caught the first dead twig; it broke under her hands, but as it broke she caught at another, and so fought her way on her hands and knees, clinging to the brittle bone-white branches, which sometimes broke and sometimes held, until she came to where Claire was wedged, unconscious, her white face thrown back, her black hair streaming on the current that frothed about her throat like a transparent robe. The child seemed to have taken on a more than human beauty, but Sylvia had no time to think of that. She could not pull Claire up to her, held in as the child was between the branches of the trunk, so she crashed her way down into the stream. Her feet touched bottom, and the icy water threw her against the barrier. The dead twigs tore her face and body, but at last she pulled the child free. By then she heard Tom shouting to her. He had worked his way out on the pine and was now sitting astride it among the first branches. Straining, panting, the blood running into her eyes, Sylvia broke her branch-beset way through to him, until he could take Claire from her, hauling her up to safety. Even without a burden, it was all that Sylvia could do to make her way to the bank. She was bruised and drained of strength when at last she took the child again from Tom, who had been edging in slowly along the trunk, carrying Claire in his arms.

This time the little girl stirred and opened her eyes, but she lay quietly as her mother carried her to the cabin, her head against Sylvia's shoulder, her long hair over her mother's arm, dripping great drops of clear water down on the winter-faded grass. Tom in his turn noticed how beautiful the child looked. But Sylvia was pale and scratched, and her eyes were both frightened and angry.

6

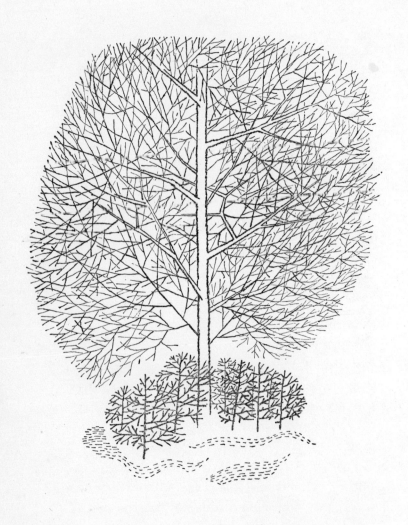

$\mathcal{E}$ARLY THE next morning when Sylvia slipped out of the cabin door, the first light of day was just brightening the snowy heights of Katahdin. Somewhere westward in clear air stood its blue impalpable shadow, and a white-throated sparrow woke and faintly, clearly, sang his thread of song.

From back of the shed came the sound of Pete Fortier splitting firewood. He worked in a leisurely way. He seldom hurried, but the pile of firewood beside him grew steadily. When he saw his daughter standing at the corner of the building looking at him, he did not stop immediately but smiled his welcome.

Between strokes of the axe, he remarked, "You're looking rather banged up, Sylvie."

"Yes," she said. "Dad, I think I'll take Claire and go down to Boston."

"For good?" He was a little surprised perhaps.

"Yes. I'll find something to do."

"Are you afraid?"

"Yes."

"I told you you had done a dangerous thing."

"Yes, but I did not realize then that it would mean Claire, too."

"But the avalanche?"

"It did not seem the same. This time she was all alone and she's so little."

"When I went in to tell her a good-night story she seemed excited, but rather pleased to have been so much the center of things."

"I've been thinking all night what was best to do."

"Did you think of going back?"

She struck her hands together.

"I can't, Dad."

"You don't love him?"

"Of course I love him! If I didn't these things wouldn't happen, I think. It's in the spring when I begin to remember; when everything wakes to life——"

"Then take my advice. Take Claire and go back."

"No, Dad. If I had always lived in the woods; if I'd never gone to Millinocket or studied geometry and European history, perhaps I could. But I'm only half you. And you yourself don't go near. Why is that? I've never asked you."

"I'm afraid to."

"But others do and nothing happens."

"All my childhood I heard the stories. None of the Indians would ever go above the timberline. But if you won't go back to him, you should marry Tom. Live in Boston winters and come back here in the summer."

"You mean that?"

"Sure. And your mother wants it. I might pass out sometime. You need a young man to look out for you and Claire, and Claire's crazy about him."

The tops of the trees were catching the light, and now they could hear Ethel Fortier moving about in the kitchen. A moment later she opened the back door and called softly, "Pete! You there? Can I have some kindling, dear?"

She was a little surprised when Sylvia came around the corner, carrying an armful.

"Didn't expect *you* up so soon," she said. "My, what a scratching you did get, didn't you? Have you tried boric acid? You ought to have put on a wrap. You're shivering, child."

Claire, too, was up before breakfast, and while she waited for the cereal to boil, she dragged her grandfather back to the house, pushed him into his big chair and climbed into his lap.

"Tell me a story," she said, leaning perilously down to drag Vicki up beside her. "Tell Vicki and me a story."

"One of my grandmother's stories, or one of my grandfather's?"

"Grandmother's! Grandmother's!"

Pete settled down and with some difficulty filled and lighted his pipe. When it was drawing well, he began.

"Once long ago an Indian girl lived all alone in her wigwam."

"Where were her father and mother?"

Sylvia, who was listening as she darned socks, laid her finger on her lips and shook her head.

"She didn't have any father or mother, but she had a grandmother like Granny Fortier. And her grandmother loved her very much, as Granny Fortier loves you, and so she would come to visit the girl, who lived in a beautiful place."

"By a stream!" Claire said decidedly.

"Yes, below a waterfall, too. It was always sunny and warm there and the trees were always green and there were lots of flowers. 'When you want to walk in the woods, you may go south,' the grandmother said, 'or east or west, but if you go north, something dreadful will happen.'

"For a long time the girl was careful to obey her grandmother, but one day she thought, 'I will go north for just a little way.' So she went north. At first nothing happened, but as she walked on, the grass seemed to turn brown and the leaves were red as fire and the wind blew cold. Then the leaves began to blow past her, and the birds flew by, and suddenly an old man appeared and took her by the hand and led her to his wigwam, which stood in a land white with snow. Her hair became white and her face old and wrinkled like his. Now she must serve the old man and the two braves who lived in his lodge and whose names were North Wind and Northeast Wind.

"But one day the girl's grandmother came again to visit her granddaughter. As she drew near she saw that no smoke was coming from the lodge. The ashes of the last fire were cold, and foxes—yes, bad, big, red foxes like Vicki— had stolen the meat, which was usually hanging from the drying stand.

" 'Mercy on us!' cried the girl's granny, just as your granny says when you're naughty. 'Mercy on us! That bad girl must have gone north, and now she can't come back to her beautiful lodge.'

"But she didn't say, 'Serves her right.' Instead, she called for her braves, just as your granny would try to help you if you were in trouble. And her two young warriors came in a minute. Their names were South Wind and Southwest Wind. And as soon as they heard what had happened, they fastened their moccasins on their feet and ran along the trail which the girl had taken, until at last they came to the lodge in the snow.

"But North Wind and Northeast Wind saw them coming and ran out to do battle. How they wrestled and struggled together! Now the old man's braves were on top, now the granny's! But after a terrible struggle it was South Wind and Southwest Wind who won, and the others ran away. When the victorious braves reached the lodge, only the old woman was there. The old man had disappeared. So they led her out and helped her along the trail towards home. And as she walked, she grew stronger and straighter. The snow melted, the bare trees were covered with buds, the buds unfolded into leaves and the birds sang among them. With every step, her hair grew longer and darker until at last when she ran to meet her granny——"

"By the stream," put in Claire, proving that she was listening.

"By the stream, she was as young and beautiful as ever, for her name was Spring and she had returned to her lodge once more."

"I don't think that's a very good story. It

wasn't scary enough," said Claire, moving restlessly.

"Well, I'll tell you about another Indian girl and this *is* scary. She lived with her tribe not far from here, but though there were many people around her, she was lonely. So one day she went out on a rock back of the village and she stretched out her arms and called out——"

" 'Breakfast's ready!' That's what she called out," Sylvia exclaimed, jumping up and beginning to put the hot cereal into the bowls.

"Let your father finish his story," her mother protested. "Porridge keeps its heat."

"But coffee doesn't," said Sylvia crisply. "Dad, put her down. She'd keep you telling stories all day."

Claire was hungry, and slipped off her grandfather's knee, and Pete obediently put out his pipe and moved to the table. But when his daughter was pouring the coffee, he gave her a quick, searching look. Her face was paler than usual, and across her high cheekbones there were superficial scratches from yesterday's experience, but he could not read the expression of her blue eyes. He guessed that she was a little angry.

When the housework was done, Sylvia took Claire to the falls, trailed by both Vicki and the cat. Yesterday's flood was now vanished away like a bad dream, leaving a few pools and heaps of debris behind. Something had excited the jays and they were crying back and forth with harsh loud shouts. But sometimes they broke the uproar with their spring calls, full and unexpectedly sweet.

As they walked on, the sound of the falls grew louder and louder through the trees, and as always Claire moved entranced. Sylvia held her hand. The danger of the day before had taught the child no fear. She was quiet, but with a quiet that Sylvia knew from experience might turn in a flash into the swiftest and most unexpected action.

They climbed to the top of the falls, only the cat walking off the path to keep out of the spray. It was too early for the twinflowers or the ghostly white moccasin flowers which they would find later, but there were little red caps, like fairy mushrooms, in the moss on old stumps, and once they saw a squirrel high up in a maple tree biting off the small twigs and sucking the sweet sap. He watched them with bright, angry eyes until at last he sprang away and nearly drowned out the music of the falls with his angry cries. Part of the trail was still covered with old snow, and all of it was slippery with mud, but Sylvia and Claire climbed easily along it, knowing every stone and twisted root that made a foothold on its course, scarcely glancing at the ground, their eyes bemused by the exulting and arrowed flight of the water beside them.

When at last it was time to return to the cabin, they found a stranger sitting by the fire with Pete and Ethel, his cigarette smoke mingling with the smoke of Pete's pipe. He was a short, thick-set man, perhaps in his late thirties, with the look of the lumberman about him, but dressed in ready-made city clothes, and wearing a wide gold ring on one heavy hand and a gold horseshoe studded with brilliants in his tie. He rose when Sylvia came in, but after they were introduced—his name was Alphonse Beaumont, he said—he paid at first little attention to her, but went on talking to her parents, to whom he was showing a Canadian catalogue of camp stoves, enlarging enthusiastically on the virtues of each type as they turned the pages at the table where they ate.

Sylvia sat down and listened with Claire beside her. At this time of the year, any visit from a stranger was a treat, and soon the child slipped away and stood watching the salesman, leaning against the table and looking more at the man than the catalogue. He began to notice her, and suddenly Sylvia too was favored with a broad wink. There was something engaging about the stranger, at once merry and crafty, the lumberjack turned city slick, but still good and naïve and cheerful at bottom.

"Well," said Pete at last, closing the catalogue. "My wife and I will have to talk it over before we make up our minds."

"Our stove is getting old," said Ethel. "It don't bake the way it used to. By the way, Mr.
——" she paused.

"Mr. Beaumont, Alphonse Beaumont," he prompted her, bowing.

"Mr. Beaumont, you'll stay for dinner. It's too late for you to get to any eating-place this morning."

"Pleased to, I'm sure," said Mr. Beaumont,

97

with another bow and a look at Sylvia, who remained silent and grave. "By the way, Mr. Fortier, from the name, I gather you're French-Canadian, like me."

The warden shook his head. "French," he agreed, "but born American. It was like this. My folks lived at Three Towns on the border and my dad's house was right on the line, more on the Canadian side than the American it was. But when I was coming along, Mama told Dad she had a fancy to move into the south room and have a little American for a change. I don't know why. It was just an idea. She had three Canadian kids already, and later she had four more, but me, I was born American. The doctor and everyone else in town knew it. I didn't have any trouble proving nationality when it came time to vote."

The women knew the story and smiled. But the stranger laughed heartily and slapped his leg.

"Don't women have ideas!" he exclaimed. "Me, I don't know where I came from. I guess I was born in a logging camp. Anyhow, I grew up in a dozen of them. Never knew my Mama or my Dad either." He threw Sylvia a look to see if

98

he had made an effect, but her expression did not change. "When I was a kid I was in these parts with a gang. You know the song?" And tilting back in his chair, he sang in a good baritone, at first low and later at the top of his lungs:

> *À la claire fontaine*
> *M'en allant promener*
> *J'ai trouvé l'eau si belle . . .*

Sylvia slipped to her feet and quietly went out, but as she closed the door the song abruptly stopped and a moment later the salesman joined her.

"What's the matter? Don't you like singing?" he asked.

"Yes, I like singing," she said, "but someone's got to put more wood in the stove."

"Let me, lady," he answered gallantly, but as she showed him where the woodpile was, behind the shed, she saw that he hesitated.

"Oh, don't get your nice shoes muddy," she said. Their eyes met, his black and lively, hers flower-blue and smiling. But behind the casual glance, the casual words, some challenge was given and accepted. For a moment they stood

99

looking at one another, in a silence filled only by the music of the falls beyond them, and then he turned and stepped off the porch into the muddy path.

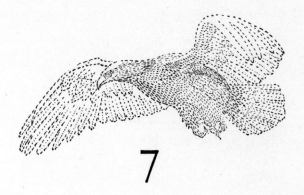

7

$\mathcal{S}$YLVIA LOOKED after the salesman as he walked away from the cabin, and as she watched him, her face came alive and her blue eyes filled with laughter and then shone with tears and her brown hands clenched at her sides until the palms were marked with the pattern of nails across them.

But when he came back with his arms filled with kindling, she stepped down into the mud and took the load like a gift into her own arms.

Her face had gone white, and now she shook her head.

"No, no," she said quietly. "You must go back where you came from. You must not come in again, Mr. Beaumont. I will make your excuses to my parents."

"But they have invited me!" he exclaimed, like a disappointed child, looking at her as though surprised. "What is wrong, Mademoiselle? I have said nothing wrong, have I? I have made no impertinence?"

She was beginning to cry, and now, turning her head away, she pointed down at the ground.

He looked, and when he laughed his voice had changed. It came from deep down in his chest and there was something primitive and earthy about it, something edged with anger and threat, yet hearty for all that, as of a man caught playing a trick, who takes it in good part, and yet will have his revenge.

He stepped towards her, but she stepped back, stumbling, her face laid almost on the kindling, curtaining it with her hair.

"No, no! Go away! Go away!"

He reached out his hand, but she still shrank

back, and then, fumbling for the door knob, she was gone into the house, closing the door in his face. He heard her speaking to her family, heard her mother protesting, and an indignant outcry from Claire, heard a few words in the deeper notes of Pete Fortier, but he did not wait. His town overshoes stood by the door and he buckled them over his shiny town shoes, and then, standing up and straightening his shoulders, turned his back on the place and walked away, thoughtfully taking out and lighting a cigarette as he went.

A few moments later Sylvia came out and stared after him until he was out of sight. She may have hoped that he would look around, but he did not turn his head. When he had disappeared among the trees, she took the path he had recently taken to the woodpile and returned with another load of wood. Before she went in, she glanced again at the route he had followed towards the road, but the earth was well drained and grassy, and there was no trace of him for her to dwell upon. As she was standing, tranced, the door burst open and Claire came out like a quicksilver fury.

"Where is he?" she stormed. "You're a horrid Mama to send him away! I'm going to bring him back!"

"He's gone," said Sylvia. When Claire began beating at her with her small fists, screaming, she laid down the kindling and catching the child's hands in one of her own, put the other over her mouth.

"Listen," she said softly. "It's the thrush. His notes are as cool as running water. And hear the falls singing with him! So quietly, so quietly."

It was the enchantment by which Claire's spirit could sometimes be chained. And now the child's angry struggles died down and she began to listen. Her mother let her go and they stood side by side, holding their breaths, their dark faces sad, intent, their eyes wet with tears. They were alike, and yet not alike. A stormier spirit moved in the child, something fierce and almost inhuman, as though her heart were a hawk's heart.

Yet when the red fox, Vicki, pawed at the door, anxious to be with her, Claire's face warmed, and she ran to let her out, and then, unable to resist the impulse to tease, held the door for a moment so that only the sharp nose could come through, which she pretended to push back, talking caressingly, before she flung the door wide open and they ran off, fox and child, creatures who lived under a roof and yet were still untamed.

Sylvia stood looking after them, forgotten as the open door was forgotten, and then, for a moment more, she looked up at the sky, which was graying over. Katahdin's crest was lost in rain. She could see the clouds' black hair streaming as the storm swept downwards. Already the trees were moving restlessly, as though afraid, with that sound which seemed to come from water, not so much the beat of breakers as the steady roar of a cataract, mingling with and subduing the music of Katahdin Falls.

It was of no use to call Claire. When she was ready to, she would come back with Vicki, both wet to the skin, diminished and dripping. Neither was ever the worse for these wettings. But still Sylvia hesitated to go in to her father's sharp glance, to her mother's questions. If only she might have looked up and found Katahdin rising above her, placid with sunshine, dreaming against a blue sky, she might have found some tranquillity for her agitated thoughts. But now her eyes saw only the coming rain, and the fretful eddying of the branches, and a world pressed low, from which no visible height lifted itself up in granite domination.

She stepped into the main room of the cabin and closed the door behind her.

"He didn't say why he had to go," she said to her mother, repeating once more an earlier conversation. "I told him that I would make his excuses. No, he didn't say when he would be back. No, he didn't speak about the catalogue. You can keep it, I guess, and write to the company."

Another year passed and Sylvia was giving Claire lessons at home, keeping in touch with the Millinocket school to which the child would ultimately go. She learned most things quickly, seizing upon knowledge as a hawk stoops to its prey, but if anything failed to interest her, she made no attempt to understand it, and would frown and look out of the window. Yet she had her own kind of patience—a long, intent waiting, or the reiterated attempt to do some hard thing which she wished to do. But she would not submit herself to dullness, and if Sylvia insisted, she would jump up from her chair, and letting books and papers fall where they would, run out with Vicki at her heels, paying no more attention than the wind to her mother's calls. Sylvia was often at her wit's end. She tried punishment, but it was like punishing a wild animal to lay hand on Claire. She tried depriving her of things, but Claire wanted little that people could give her, and if her mother shut her up in her room, she either dropped out of the window or screamed herself into exhaustion.

"You can never break her," Pete Fortier said to his daughter one day after such a scene. "She herself is the only person she will ever obey. You must find a way to make her wish to control herself."

"And what way would that be?" Sylvia asked wearily.

"That I don't know," said her father. "But I do know that you are wasting your time trying to do your duty by your child. She lives by her own laws."

After that, Sylvia did indeed almost give up trying to discipline Claire, and there was less tension in the cabin, although Ethel Fortier often made clear what she felt about a grand-daughter of hers being allowed to grow up like a savage. Her earlier blind subjection to Claire was long past, and now she was critical of every-thing that the child did or said, and constantly remarked upon her conduct to Sylvia.

"I don't suppose it matters what I think," she would begin, or "Now, if I stood in your shoes," or "When I was young, no little girl in the world would have dared," and so on, and when Sylvia only sighed, her mother returned to her old crocheting, into which she was pouring her wan-ing forces with increasing frenzy, so that now she was half through a pattern of Leonardo da Vinci's "Last Supper" in ecru.

Only Pete Fortier appeared to accept Claire just as she was, and she rewarded him by placing him next to Vicki in her affections. Like Sylvia when a child, she often went into the woods with him, and he taught her the lore of trail and thicket, or tried to teach her, for most things she seemed to know by feral instinct like a young animal. She saw things which he missed, heard sounds which never reached his ears, and could outdistance him on any trail, which was perhaps not surprising since he was now past fifty. He loved most of all to watch her on a down-trail. She was perfectly surefooted and perfectly fearless, and the more headlong the descent the better she liked it. He would see her light dress flashing downwards from rock to rock in an ecstasy of release, and when at last he would catch up to her, he would find her waiting for him in the happiest and mildest mood. It was characteristic of Claire that she did not care much for snowshoeing and would leave Sylvia and her grandfather any time to go skiing with Tom.

Tom Ellison still came to the cabin and still made love to Sylvia, but now he as often told her of his affairs with other girls. He had been engaged more than once, but something always seemed to happen. At times, the girls changed their minds, as the trees changed their summer green to autumn red, but one or twice it was Tom who at the last moment turned hard and cold, and broke off.

"He's still hoping to have *you*," Ethel Fortier would declare. "You're old enough now to stop behaving like a school girl. Mr. Ola, whoever he was, has never come back. You can get a divorce for desertion, if you were ever married, which I doubt."

"But I'm not in love with Tom."

"The more fool you!" her mother would exclaim bridling. "Tom is a civilized human being, which is more than I can say of the people in this household, even your father."

But whenever Ethel spoke of Pete her voice changed. The words might be critical, but she could not keep her voice from softening and warming at mention of him. For so many years now he had stood between her and the wilderness, and his watchful protection had never weakened. If she had left behind her in the villages everything which she had valued, she had this instead, and it sufficed.

The spring following Claire's tenth birthday was a very rainy one. The snow melted early, the ice went out of the ponds a fortnight before the usual time, and the pair of eagles that had for so long cruised the sky on that side of the mountain were back on their airy watchtowers sooner than ever before. Day and night sounded with the dripping of water. Falling from the sky, sluicing off the mountain, sliding from the roofs, trickling through the mosses, dripping from the branches, the sweet monotonous sounds seemed never to stop, and Katahdin Falls exulted over and under all the thousand watery murmurs and trillings and tappings which filled the air. The cabin smelled damp; things were clammy to the touch.

"It rains easy," said Pete, standing at the open door. He went about his work as usual, but he didn't like so much rain. Ethel complained of the mud tracked in on her floors, and Sylvia grew quieter, receding into the patience which was her fortress. Only Claire was happy, and went about singing little murmurs of song, which came out of her own head. She was wild, too, leaping out of the door with Vicki after her, and making off into the sweet wet woods whenever she had the chance.

"Botheration!" she cried the morning she woke up to find sunshine at the windows.

"It's a lovely day," her grandmother rebuked her. "See how the grass sparkles!"

And the Beasts of the Apocalypse, who had

been looming up over against the cabin on the wild nights of rain, lay down again in their dens, their strange jaws upon their paws and their fiery eyes closed in sleep. Now once again the mountains brought peace to the people and the Lord no longer came down "like rain upon the mown grass; as showers that water the earth."

"Why don't we go on a picnic?" Sylvia suggested. "Dad, how far off is the deers' graveyard? Couldn't we go there? It will be much drier in an hour or two."

Earlier that year Pete had come upon a place filled with the bones and antlers of deer, which fitted in with old stories he had heard from hunters and guides of how sick or wounded deer go off somewhere to die. No one whom he knew had found it before. Ever since he had told his family about the deers' graveyard, Sylvia had wanted to go there and even Ethel's curiosity had been touched, but he had said it was too far.

"I blazed a trail, but it's rough. I'll work on it this summer, Ethel, and take you there in the fall. It's quite a sight."

In the end they went to The Knob, a rocky knee of the mountain from which they could look a long way out over the forest and the shattered brightness of lakes and the breathing rise and fall of cloud-shadowed lesser mountains. Katahdin Stream sounded from the base of the rock, and the spring sun warmed the granite and set into motion the thousand, thousand little lives which ran across it or lay in wait in its cracks or settled down upon its pinnacles, resting new, barely unfolded wings.

Pete chose a low boulder and spread a blanket there for Ethel to sit on, while Sylvia laid out the picnic on a cloth which she had carried in a pack on her back. As usual in the spring, she was in a preoccupied and brooding mood, not always hearing when she was spoken to, not always answering if she heard. Her eyes came back with difficulty to the object before them, and her wide mouth had a patient downward droop. For her these were weeks of twilight and shadow when the daily life of the cabin became unreal and her face took on a haunted and haunting beauty. Her gaze was most often on Claire, who was exploring The Knob with Vicki. On one side there was a cliff along which they threaded their way fearlessly, bright and young and sunlit against the new green of the forest beyond.

"Claire!" Sylvia called when the pack was at last empty. "Claire! Come along! We're ready to eat!"

But Claire paid no attention. Pete slipped away before Sylvia could call again, and joining the child, was soon deep in talk with her, leading her back to the spread cloth as they talked. Arrived at the food, she gave the women a sudden mischievous smile and throwing herself down on the rock, began to eat without waiting for the others, stopping only to tear the sliced chicken and ham out of sandwiches to throw to Vicki, who waited beside her with sharp ears pricked forward.

"Stop that this minute!" her grandmother exclaimed. "There won't be enough for the rest of us! Vicki's dinner is in the green bowl." But Claire went on as though she had not heard.

It was at this moment that the big yellow dog appeared, coming down the trail. He seemed to have travelled a long way. His coat was matted and his tail hung low and he trotted as though all the pads of his feet were worn thin. When he saw people he stopped, raised his head, wagged his tail uncertainly, and then approached, his lips drawn back ingratiatingly, his yellow gaze moving from person to person.

"Poor creature!" Ethel exclaimed. "He's lost and half-starved. You'll have to drive down to Millinocket with him, Pete. Come, doggie, come, doggie!" and she put Vicki's bowl down on the rock towards the dog, which still hesitated, weaving its heavy mastiff-like body as it approached, crawling close to the ground as though to humble itself before them.

"Hold on to Vicki," Pete called to Claire, getting up himself to go over to the fox. Sylvia too had jumped up, and as she passed by the dog, a bowl of powdered sugar still in her hand spilled its contents onto the rock and before it could draw back, the dog had walked across it.

Standing between the animal and the child, Sylvia turned.

"Go away!" she said angrily to the dog, as though it would understand. "Go away and don't come back!"

The creature stopped and there was no hint now of its former fawning. Raised up to its full height, its yellow eyes blazing, it looked more like a mountain lion than a dog. For a moment it seemed about to spring on the girl, but just then Vicki, who had never seen a dog before, ran forward inquisitively, reaching up to touch noses with the great intruder.

With a snarl, the dog fastened its teeth in Vicki's red ruff of fur, but before he could do more, Claire, with a shriek, had flashed into battle.

When Claire fought, she fought as an animal fights, instinctively and savagely using her strength where the enemy was weakest. Now she struck with her fists at the dog's eyes. Under the rain of blows, the great animal was forced to turn its head. By now Sylvia was trying to pull Claire away, but the child had a maniacal strength, and before Pete could get into action, the dog dropped Vicki and caught the little girl by one bare forearm, sinking its teeth into the flesh and holding on.

As Vicki fled, Claire stopped screaming and beating at her assailant's head. Now she stood still, with her arm in the dog's jaws. She was perfectly unafraid. In the queer silence, which even

118

Ethel did not break, the child and dog stared at one another, and almost the same fiery pride was in their eyes.

Then slowly, unhurriedly, the dog loosened its grip and Claire's arm dropped to her side. She did not move away, and for a moment more the dog, too, stood its ground, staring at the child. Next its yellow gaze swung to Sylvia, who had straightened and now gazed somberly back at the animal. Then, without a glance at the others, it turned about and trotted up the trail and out of sight.

Ethel was shaking and white.

"You'll have to shoot it, Pete," she said. "Pity you didn't have your gun with you! It seemed so friendly, didn't it? We must get right back and put antiseptic on Claire's arm. You don't suppose it was mad, Pete?"

"No, Ethel, he wasn't mad. Claire's all right."

Claire would scarcely stand still to let them look at her arm, which was bleeding. The marks of the four canine teeth were four deep holes in the smooth skin, four small and welling fountains.

"I'll climb down and wash off the blood," Claire said. And she whistled to Vicki.

"That dog may still be around," Ethel Fortier objected, looking about her uneasily, but Pete thought they'd seen the last of him.

"You'll have to go after him, Pete, he'll be running deer." But Pete only nodded absently.

"No, don't worry, dear. The dog's all right."

He was glancing at Sylvia, who had turned away, but he could see her shoulders, and for a wonder, Claire looked at her mother too.

Suddenly she ran to her and threw her arms around her waist, careless of the blood, which reddened Sylvia's shirt.

"Don't cry, Mother," she whispered. "He didn't hurt me. Don't cry, Mother."

Sylvia bent down to her child as a birch bends in a wind, and for a moment they clung together. For a moment the brooding heart and the wild heart beat together. For a moment they were of one flesh and of one blood, true mother and daughter, but only for a moment.

Then Claire stirred impatiently, and quickly Sylvia let her go, straightening as a birch straightens when the gust of wind passes, and quick and sure Claire was off, with Vicki running by her side, finding a path where there was no path down the cliff, now moving sideways, now leaping downwards, now pausing, now darting until she had made her way to the stream.

Sylvia had wiped her eyes and was quietly packing the picnic things. Once she looked up to find her father standing where the dog had stood, looking down at the whiteness of powdered sugar, still lodged in the cracks of granite. But the breeze had blown the light sugar about in its eddies, and now it had re-formed like a thin mist. Seeing her eyes on him, Pete looked uncomfortable and went over to help his wife to her feet.

"I get so stiff sitting."

"You're not used to sitting on rock. Perhaps this sort of picnic is a little too much for you."

Ethel smiled, her eyes bright blue in the sunlight.

"I don't mind. I like it. But I hope next time there won't be another dog." The Beasts, the great Beasts of the Apocalypse, suddenly woke in their dens, and stirred. Had this been one of them, with its golden eyes? At first she had been sorry for it, a lost dog strayed into the reservation, likely to be shot by the first ranger it met

121

with, unless Pete would take it out and find somewhere for it to stay. But afterwards it hadn't seemed like a lost dog, just Beast. It had looked about it, as though it wore a golden crown on its head and could prophesy the fall of nations.

Ethel gave herself a little shake. She knew her fancies were dangerous. She mustn't imagine things. A yellow dog is a yellow dog. Everything would have been all right if only that child had held on to her fox as she had been told. Maybe she'd learn something now and do as she was bid once in a while, but Ethel doubted it.

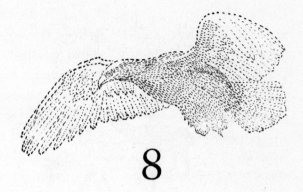

8

$\mathcal{I}$T WAS about ten days later that Sylvia decided to go to the deers' cemetery. The others, down to Vicki on a leash, had all driven to town to buy supplies, but Sylvia had no desire to go with them. She was often alone at the cabin, but today her father seemed anxious.

"You go down and see how Tom's getting on at the camp," he suggested. "Maybe you can help him. He's short of hands this spring."

"Maybe I will."

"You do, Sylvia. I don't like to leave you alone."

Sylvia laughed.

"I've been alone here since I was ten years old."

"You go down and see Tom," he urged.

She had not said yes or no, and Ethel had already started for the road and the car. As for Claire and Vicki, no one could say where they were, but they would be on hand before the old Ford was pointed towards Millinocket.

"You be careful," he repeated, lingering still. "Sylvia, I don't like it."

She ran to where he was standing and put her hand on his arm.

"Don't you worry, Dad," she said affectionately. "I'm all right. In all these years has anything hurt me?"

"Not yet, but nearer than I like."

"You're as bad as Mother." She laughed at him. "Now go along, Dad. I'm all right."

But when they were all gone, Sylvia decided to see if she could find the deers' graveyard.

"One place is like another," she said to herself. "I can't allow myself to be afraid," and she started off alone, taking a light axe with her to make a first clearing of the trail as she went along.

She knew where the path started, and she was
so accustomed to her father's methods of blazing
that she followed without much difficulty. Sometimes the trail led through more or less open
forest, where her feet sank in the moss. Sometimes she had to make her way under or over a
windfall, and sometimes she paused at a thicket
to work for a while lopping branches or young
trees until the path was clear. Now and then a
partridge drummed up from the underbrush,
and in some places the white-throated sparrows
were singing, bird answering bird unseen among
the branches. Once she stopped to listen to an
olive-backed thrush and once she paused to look
down at a mass of flicker feathers, the yellow as
bright as buttercups and quite unstained by
blood. Yet death was here, too, even among the
birds, which seemed to have the radiancy of im-
mortal spirits. They only appeared to be above
sorrow and pain. In danger of their lives, they
held their little kingdoms, challenging their
equals from tree to tree, defending their open
nests. In danger of their lives they raised their
young and in ceaseless labor fed them. And in the
starkest danger of all they forced them to their
independence, urging them out of the nest, en-

couraging them, entreating them to try their
muscleless wings, and if all else failed, forcing
them over the rim of safety and so to the des-
perate flutter and fall, ending on the perilous
earth from which they must soon learn to fly up,
or die, a prey to all the dangers that stalk along
the ground.

Once or twice Sylvia lost the way, and beat
back and forth until she again picked up the
blazes. She skirted a small pond, walking in soft
muck that stank as her feet opened its secret
darkness. The frogs were booming "jug o' rum,
jug o' rum" from the reeds along one shore, and
a dead fish floated, belly up, among the water-
lily leaves. Here she could see the sky and the
free clouds passing overhead, and Katahdin's
heights colored the surface of the water with
reflections of their stone. Again the forest closed
green above her, and she followed the blazes
through whole gardens of different-colored toad-
stools and fallen beech trees fringed with fungi.
For nearly a mile, her way led through forest
killed by some long-ago fire. The bark had
peeled from the dead trees, which stood like
skeletons, most of their branches fallen away,

but some, with what seemed like arms and hands white as bone, were posturing against the blue sky; and here a flock of crows was clamoring, harrying a small hawk, like the members of a rabble hunting down and by their numbers overpowering one of their masters caught alone, armed but helpless among them.

It was at this point that Sylvia almost turned back. Something about this whole nation of dead trees moved and frightened her. She hesitated, took a few steps in the direction from which she had come, and then stopped and stood for a little while perfectly still, collecting herself. When she moved, it was forward along the unknown trail. After a while she could see green through the dead trunks, and broke almost into a run until she had put the desolation behind her.

It was not long after this that she came once more to open sky, but this time it was a slide of rocks that she had to pass. At some time, perhaps in an earlier geological age, there had been a great landslide down the side of Katahdin. All about her lay the savage jumble of stone, tilted and tipped in every direction, sometimes forming granite caves or upraised like old tombs roofed over with thatches of green ferns. Here trees had thrust their way only occasionally. In some places her father had marked the trail by heaps of smaller stones. Walking was difficult in that rent and savage place, where the danger was that the thin earth would give way to catch the foot in a trap between two rocks. Sylvia passed close to a cave in the ledges with a half-eaten rabbit before it. She must have frightened the fox family away, and they had retreated into the earth, leaving dinner on the table. Now in silence and darkness they must be scenting the air to learn more of the intruder, and their pointed ears would be listening to discover if she stopped to rob them of their deserted feast.

But on went Sylvia, with only a glance. Behind her she knew that eyes would be watching. Ahead of her, eyes retreated. She moved, the center of a circle of fierce or timid eyes, of held breaths, of silent footfalls, as predator and prey moved back to make room for her. Gentle and pitying, she moved among them, but they knew her for what she was, the daughter of Man, the Killer of Killers, the ultimate death.

It was not long after she had worked her way through the rockslide that she came to the place that her father had described. It was not exactly a clearing, but there were few trees growing there, for the ground was marshy, and surrounded by thickets almost impenetrable except where they were pierced by ancient game trails. At first glance the earth seemed covered by old branches and twigs, such as one may find along the shores of forest lakes, but as Sylvia looked more closely she saw that they were antlers mixed with a few other bones, the browned ribs which had once caged living hearts, the thigh and leg bones once swift in flight, the shield-shaped foreheads which had once met armed shield to shield in battle for a mate. Mostly these bones had been dragged about by long-ago predators, but the marrowless horns lay piled about here and there like trophies, both grim and beautiful.

She was not surprised when she saw someone coming towards her. Perhaps she had always known that he would be there, and now she went to meet him across the valley of bones. He was as she had first seen him, a young man, with straight hair and black eyes, with brows that frowned and a smiling mouth. He was dressed, too, as she first remembered him, in mackinaw, corduroy trousers and laced boots, and at sight of him it seemed to her that all the joys and pains that she had ever known struggled together in her heart, which was too small to hold them. And above her bannered heart, the small cold citadel of her mind warned her, "Be careful. Be careful. He is dangerous."

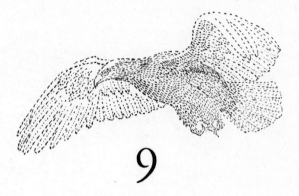

9

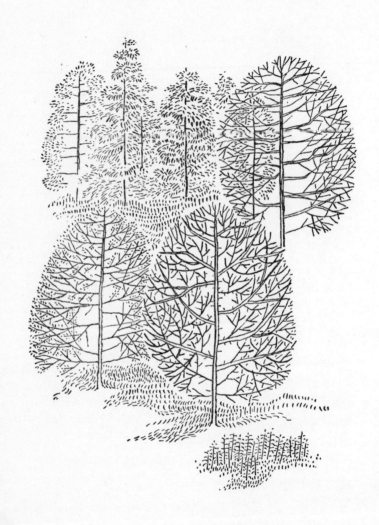

*T*HEY STOOD facing one another, staring. Then he held out his arms.

"My Sylvie," he said, and she came to him on quick light feet. Once again she heard through all her veins the strong hammering of his heart, once again she was trapped and upheld in his arms, once again she felt his kisses and returned them, her face raised to his, her soft dark hair blown back across his arm.

For a long time they said nothing, each lost in the moment, but at last they moved a little apart and with his arm about her waist sat down side by side on a log. He said:

"Do you remember the first time? You sent for me half in sport, and you didn't believe that I would come. And when I came, you did not believe that I was I, but you went with me just the same."

> " 'Pamóla, I am lonely.
> I am here. I am waiting for you.
> Come to me, Pamóla, from the
> crest of Katahdin.
> I am not afraid of storms
> nor of lightning.
> I am not afraid of thunder
> nor blizzard,
> Come to me, Pamóla,
> gently and tenderly.
> I am waiting; I am young and lonely.'

"That was what I said, wasn't it? I was remembering Dad's old stories of how an Indian girl once called you and you answered her. I was wondering what she had said."

"I came to you as I came to her. The Indian hunters feared me, so I killed them if they dared climb my mountain. But you called me and didn't fear me. Why did you go away? I have sent for you, but you would not come. Again and again I have sent my messengers and come in disguise, but you mocked us. This time I have come as I came to you first."

"I could not go back to the cave."

"Could not? You, a girl down here in a ranger's cabin, whom I took up into the hollow lodge of Katahdin, whom I held in my arms? Is not the heart of the mountain enough for you? What do you ask for, you blue-eyed Indian?"

"I don't want to talk about it."

"I want you to come back with me. I have missed you and longed for you. There has been night in my heart ever since you left."

"I cannot come."

"And you are to bring the child. She is my child and yours. I felt a father's pride when she did not flinch when I was a dog and tested her courage with my teeth. She will like it in my lodge. I will teach her to raise storms and blast with lightning. She's fierce, that one. You are like a dove, and I will cherish you. But she is a young eagle and she will be my pride."

"No! No! Claire is never to go near that place. Be as angry as you like. She is not to go to the mountain."

They had moved away from one another on the log and swung about now face to face. Sylvia's hands were locked together, but her blue eyes were big and steady to meet his frown.

"And why?" he asked haughtily. "No, no, I do not wish to hear. I am not accustomed to allow mortals to criticize the way I live."

"You are a spirit, Pamola, and I love you. But the heights are too much for a woman. I tried, oh, I tried, but I could not, any more than a tree can live above the timberline."

"You were happy the first days."

"Oh, yes! Yes! You will never believe how happy I was! But you were in the shape you have now, and the bones just lay along the wall of the cave. You brought me there in a moment, like an eagle. I closed my eyes with my arms about your neck and then I could feel the wind whipping by me and I knew that you were a spirit. I was so proud to be loved by you. And you were gentle to me. All day we wandered in the sunshine with the world misty at our feet, in a dream of forests and lakes."

"Well. I can be like that. I will be like that again, Sylvie. I will wear this shape, I will sing you songs, sitting on the highest rock of the mountain."

"But then some night it will happen again."

"What of that? I have many aspects. A wife should honor them all."

She stood up and beat her hands together.

"Yes, yes, Pamola. A wife should honor them all. But I can't. I can't. Do you understand? I can't make myself. When the bones began to beat on the drums and the skeletons rose up to dance, and then you appeared, you, in whose arms I had slept, and I saw that you were only part man——"

"What is wrong about the moose? And surely there is nothing nobler than an eagle?"

"No, no, Pamola! They are noble, of course. But I was only a young girl. And I thought that you were a young man who happened also to be an Indian spirit. I hadn't taken the old tales literally. I didn't know that you had three natures and three appearances and that they were mixed together. When I saw you dancing with your eagle feet——"

Pamola looked down at his well-polished

walking boots and smiled for the first time since they had been talking.

"But you will admit that you find it convenient to know that my feet always leave the print of an eagle? Twice you found me out because of that. If I could have tasted your father's food, you would have been in my power."

She smiled; it was a wary smile, matching his.

"Oh, yes," she said, "it is convenient."

"Now for the third and last time I have come in person to ask you to come back. What is it that you want, Sylvie? I have had many reports of you from my messengers. Do you want to marry again?"

"No. I could love no other man after loving you. I have had the best—yes, and the worst. Now I want to be left alone to bring up Claire. If only Claire were more human, nearer to me, I should ask for nothing more of life."

"Sylvie, Sylvie, come back to me."

"No. I cannot. I could forget my fear of the howling wind and the thunder of the drums and the creaking and crackling of the skeletons, although some day I would be one of them. No, I could resign myself even to that. But not to you, Pamola. Not to your three natures. I can't."

"You were afraid?"

"I was disgusted."

Now it was he who sprang from his seat and stood furiously facing her.

But when he spoke, his voice was cold and calm, although the veins were beating in his forehead.

"I shall not ask you again," he said. "This is the last time you will see me. I will leave these valleys and go back to my home on the heights where I belong. You are right, Sylvie. A spirit cannot match with a human. You can lift her body to your lodge, but not her soul. She cannot understand the nature and presence of a spirit. You have meant Spring and love to me, Sylvie, and I shall not forget you. One of my natures will always be lonely for you, but I shall not come again."

She was crying now.

"I shall be lonely for you all my life."

"Having three natures, I cannot shed two of them as a deer may shed its horns, just to please you, Sylvie. But before I go, I will leave a gift for our daughter. I give her three times the power to curse, and three times the power to bless."

"Don't give her any gifts!" she wailed. "Let her alone. If you must give gifts, give them to me."

"Oh, you," he said, and now his voice had turned harsh. "Since you ask for gifts, this is my gift to you!"

She saw him coming towards her and now he stood twice the height of a man and clothed in the symbols of his three natures. His eyes burned, and as he raised his hand it was bright as lightning descending upon her. The buffet struck her to the ground, the pain of it seared along her cheek, but she struggled immediately back upon her feet to face him.

There was nothing to face. He had vanished, and only the antlers of long-dead deer raised their crooked prongs about her wherever she looked.

So this was their farewell.

The family returned from Millinocket at about five o'clock and found the cabin empty. Pete, suppressing his alarm, hurried down to the camp, but she had not been seen there. After a while he thought of the trail to the deers' burying-ground and found the signs of her work along it. Telling Ethel that he would be back soon, he took his revolver and flashlight without letting his wife see what he was doing, and forbidding Claire to follow him, set off with apparent casualness. But once in the shelter of the woods, Pete broke into a run. Steadily he hurried on as the twilight deepened, following easily the signs of her recent passing, the white scars of branches on the trees, and the heaps of piled foliage beside the trail.

He found Sylvia in the burned-over forest, lying beside the path, under a skeleton pine, half asleep, half fainting, wholly exhausted. He brought her to, and helped her back, asking no questions, sometimes half carrying her. But near the cabin she rallied, washed her face and hands, kneeling at the edge of Katahdin Stream, reached up and straightened her hair and clothes and with her hand under his arm walked onto the porch with a firm step and so into the house.

Claire and Vicki were not in sight, but Ethel

Fortier was there in her rocking chair. She looked up at them from the Bible on her knee.

"Well," she began, "I was beginning to worry."

She broke off, staring.

"Sylvie, my baby girl, what has happened to you?"

"It's all right, Mother," Sylvia said. "I've played with fire and I've been burned."

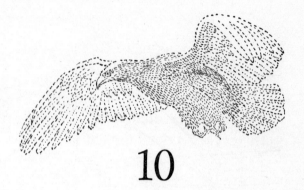

10

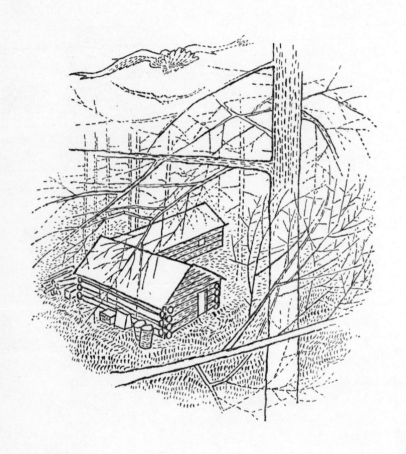

THE SCAR on Sylvia's cheek did not go away. It remained as Ethel Fortier had first seen it, a red mark that ran in a zigzag like lightning from brow to chin, blasting her beauty, but in return giving her face an air of destined tragedy and strength. When Claire first saw it, she cried wildly on her mother's shoulder, patting the cheek as though to heal it of this horror. But soon the household became used to this new Sylvia, and it was as though she had never been different.

Tom Ellison came, and only his eyes flinched

at his first sight of the ruin. He proposed that very afternoon, but it was his last proposal. After that he did not find his way up to the cabin very often, and the next fall he married a lively girl from Georgia who talked incessantly and was actually as practical and hardheaded as she appeared diaphanous and scatterbrained.

But long before that time, Claire discovered the nature of the gifts which had been made her. It was in early June, when the northern lilac by the cabin's back door was in bloom and the twinflowers were beginning to come out in the woods, that the trouble began.

Claire was very fond of marzipan, and her grandfather, coming back from town, had brought her a brightly colored candy peach, which she had left on a low table while she ran out with the others to see a box turtle which Pete had just found on the lawn.

When they all came back into the cabin, there was Vicki finishing up the last of the marzipan peach. Claire, who was almost never angry with Vicki, now flew into one of her passions.

"I hope it chokes you!" she screamed. "I hope it chokes you!"

Vicki looked at her quizzically, her pointed head a little on one side. Then, all of a sudden, she began to make strangling sounds in her throat, fell down on her side, struggled back to her feet, fell again, and lay still.

"Oh, Vicki, Vicki," moaned the little girl, kneeling beside her.

"Quick!" cried her mother. "You must wish a good wish as soon as you can!"

"I wish that you weren't dead, Vicki," Claire sobbed, and the fox began to stir and her eyes looked again at her mistress, but still the choking sounds went on.

"Can I wish again, Mother?"

"Yes. But be careful. Don't waste your wishes."

"I wish that you were as well as you were when you were a young, young fox," and scarcely had the sound of the words fallen into silence than Vicki was on her feet again and her coat seemed brighter and longer and her tail bushier and her expression livelier than anyone could remember. The two women sat down.

"What is it, Mother?" Claire said in a low voice, climbing into her mother's lap, a thing she very seldom did. "Why should Vicki fall down when I said so, and get up like that? I don't understand."

"Your father has given you the power to curse three times and to bless three times."

"When?"

"When he touched my cheek."

The child sat a long time thinking this over. She did not ask who her father was. She may have known by other means than they understood, or she may not even have wondered, but taken him for granted as children take so much.

"And I've used up one of my curses and two of my blessings?"

"Yes."

Ethel, with Pete's quieting hand upon her shoulder, had watched and listened in thunderstruck silence, looking from speaker to speaker and once or twice running the tip of her tongue over her lips as though trying herself to speak. The mystery of her daughter's life was a little clearer, but still it loomed so vague and unnamable that she, companioned though she was by the Apocalyptic Beasts, turned her thoughts quickly away to the firmer ground of curses and blessings, so much a part of her reading and meditations. Now she broke in, speaking in a high voice, with elderly authority.

"The thing for Claire to do is to go out and curse some of the crows and use her curses up. With a temper like hers, two curses are like two sticks of dynamite. She might kill anybody, anytime."

"She wants to think it over," said Pete. "A curse like that would be very convenient if a bear happened to get ugly."

"Hush!" said Claire. "I'm thinking. Mother, was it from my father that I got my temper?"

"Perhaps."

"And he did that thing to your cheek?"

"Yes."

"Was he angry?"

"Oh, I think so."

No one spoke, and after a moment Ethel Fortier bit her lip and picked up her sewing. Vicki had been playing with an empty spool, batting it daintily along the floor first with one black paw and then with another, but now she lay down, heaved a sigh and closed her eyes.

"Grandma says I might kill someone."

"You still have one good wish."

"But after that I have only a bad wish."

"Perhaps you might use up one bad wish on the crows and keep the other."

"Let me think."

Something was changing in the atmosphere of that room with its many windows outlined by chintz curtains, its stone fireplace with Ethel's crocheted eagle over the mantel, its long table which Pete himself had made, and its Indian rugs along the floor. Just as a coming change in weather may make itself felt, or a sickness will send out symptoms as heralds before it puts in its appearance, so now something new of the spirit was being born in the cabin. Pete sat down beside his wife and lighted his pipe, watching from the ambush of its smoke; Ethel, excited and bewildered, stuck her needle in and out of the cloth, in and out, wanting to burst into questions and admonitions but held back by a sense of something beyond speech which her talk would only break through; Vicki retreated from the tension into sleep; and Sylvia, with her arms loosely about Claire, waited for what was to come.

A long time went by. The hornets at the

window, the clock on the mantel made their small sounds, Ethel's chair creaked and was silent. A bird uttered a few anxious notes. There was a rustle among the lilac leaves at the back door, Vicki stirred and struck a velvet paw sideways against the floor. But the sense of waiting never lightened. The invisible change went on, the slow, silent, and mortal struggle.

When Claire slipped from her mother's lap and said, "I'll keep them all," the breathing in the room changed and Vicki opened her eyes and raised her head.

"Do you understand what that means?" Sylvia asked painfully, as though after the long silence she found it difficult to speak.

But Claire was prodding Vicki awake with her bare foot.

"Of course," she said, as she might have spoken of taking a sweater with her on a cold day or any other triviality. "Let's not talk about it any more. Come on, Vicki," and in a flash she was gone out the door, closing it behind her.

"Nobody tells me what's happening," Ethel complained, released by the sound of the closing door.

"Did you see her eyes, Dad?"

"Yes. They were quite different. She has accepted the responsibility for herself. From now on she'll be all right."

"I can't make head or tail out of what you're saying," Ethel began, biting off a thread; but already Sylvia had slipped out of the house. There was no sign of Claire and the fox; they had vanished like water under the leaves, but she was not looking for them. Her eyes went to the crest of Katahdin in the late light of afternoon. The granite peak stood up against the sky as though its real business was with the clouds and the constellations, the sun and the moon, the lightning and the wind, not with the folds of wilderness from which it had risen. Over her head passed the two eagles, flying together, one a little behind the other, strong and unhurried. She watched them until the white of their great tails caught the light like two stars, and then they were lost somewhere in the shadow of the mountain.

Sylvia's hand touched her cheek.

"You knew what gifts were best for us," she said, to herself and to more than herself. "Though we may never meet again, between us there can be no farewell."